This Little Tiger book belongs to:

_____

_____

_____

To Ann, who can out-hug anyone!
~ S S

For the kids – Fluff, Kangaroo and the
Mole Brothers et al ~ T W

LITTLE TIGER PRESS
1 The Coda Centre, 189 Munster Road, London SW6 6AW
www.littletiger.co.uk

First published in Great Britain 2006
as *Bumbletum*
This edition published 2016

A CIP catalogue record for this book is available
from the British Library

Printed in China • LTP/1800/1760/1216
2 4 6 8 10 9 7 5 3 1

A Hug For Humphrey

Steve Smallman

Illustrated by Tim Warnes

LITTLE TIGER PRESS
London

There was a new toy
in the bedroom. He was
small, soft and floppy
and had a squidgy tummy
covered in stripes.
His name was Humphrey.

"Hello," said Milly Mouse. "What sort of toy are you?" Humphrey thought very hard then said, "This sort."

"And what can you do?" asked Edgar the teddy bear.

Humphrey thought even harder. "Something good," he said, "but I don't know what it is yet."

"We'll help you to find out!" said the toys.

"You look a bit like a mouse," said Milly. "Can you squeak like this?"
SQUEAK! SQUEAK!

Humphrey tried and Milly
helped, but nothing happened.

"You look a bit like a teddy bear," said Edgar. "Can you make a growly noise when you bend over like this?" GROWL! GROWL!

GROWL! GROWL!

Humphrey tried and
Edgar helped, but
nothing happened.

"Your tail is a bit like mine," said Pip the puppy. "Can you wag it like this?" WIGGLE WAGGLE! WIGGLE WAGGLE!

Humphrey tried
but instead of
wiggling and
waggling he
just wibbled and
wobbled . . .

and fell over.

Then another toy came over. It was Tilly Tinkler, the baby doll. "Can you wet yourself like this?" she asked, and TINKLE TINKLE! she made a little puddle.

Humphrey was very impressed.
He tried and tried and tried, but
nothing happened.

Humphrey was worn out. He flopped down on the floor and had a little think. "I must be a 'doesn't really do anything' sort of toy," he said sadly.

But the other toys were sure there was something Humphrey could do.

"I know!" cried Boomer the kangaroo, bounding over. "It's your tummy!" he said excitedly.

"My tummy?" said Humphrey.

"It's stripy like a bumblebee, and what can bumblebees do?"

"Buzz?" asked Humphrey.

"FLY!" said Boomer, and the others all agreed.

Milly and Boomer helped
Humphrey up on to the bed.
"Now, when you're ready,
JUMP!" the toys all shouted.

But Humphrey
wasn't ready. The bed
was very high and the floor was
a very long way down. His knees started
to shake and his tummy felt all wibbly.
 "I'M NOT A BEE!" he cried, "AND I DON'T
THINK I'M SUPPOSED TO FLY!"

Boomer decided to help.
"Try bouncing a bit first,
like this!" he said.
BOING! BOING!
Then Milly joined in.
They bounced up and
down, up and down,
getting higher and
higher.

BOING!

BOING!

"LOOK, HUMPHREY! I'M
FLYING!" Milly squeaked,
but then . . .

. . . BOING! THUMP! SQUEAK! Milly fell off the bed and landed in a heap on the carpet.

"DON'T WORRY, MILLY, I'M COMING!" Humphrey called as he slid down the duvet to land flump on the floor.

He scooped Milly up in his arms and gave her a BIG hug.

Humphrey's tummy was so soft and snuggly that Milly felt better almost at once, but she stayed a bit longer just to be sure.

"Thank you, Humphrey," she sighed. "That's the best hug I've ever had!"

"HUGGING!" Humphrey cried. "THAT'S WHAT I CAN DO! Who wants a hug?"

The toys all hurried over and settled down in a cosy heap with Humphrey right in the middle. And although Humphrey still didn't know what sort of toy he was, he knew it must be something very special indeed!

WIGGLE WAGGLE!

More fabulous books from Little Tiger Press!

I'm Special, I'm Me!
Ann Meek
Sarah Massini

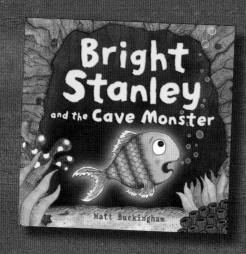

Bright Stanley and the Cave Monster
Matt Buckingham

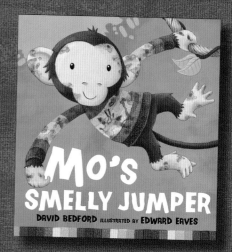

Mo's SMELLY JUMPER
DAVID BEDFORD ILLUSTRATED BY EDWARD EAVES

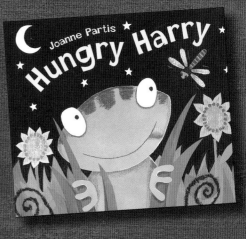

Hungry Harry
Joanne Partis

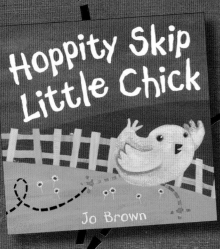

Hoppity Skip Little Chick
Jo Brown

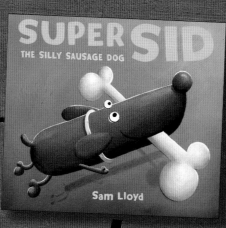

SUPER SID THE SILLY SAUSAGE DOG
Sam Lloyd

For information regarding any of the above titles
or for our catalogue, please contact us:
Little Tiger Press, 1 The Coda Centre,
189 Munster Road, London SW6 6AW
Tel: 020 7385 6333
E-mail: contact@littletiger.co.uk
www.littletiger.co.uk